Puss in Boots

ILLUSTRATED BY JAN NESBITT

Story adapted by
Christine Deverell

Once upon a time there lived a poor miller who had three sons. When he died, all he owned was divided between his sons; the eldest had the mill, the second son had the donkey and cart, and all that was left

for the youngest son was the miller's black cat. The boy was very fond of the cat, but could not see how she would ever make his fortune.

As he stroked her gently, she said, "Don't worry, master. If you do what I tell you, you will see what I can do for you. First, get me a large bag and a pair of boots." The miller's son took the last few shillings he had, and bought the cat a large bag and a pair of yellow boots.

The cat put on her new boots and went out into the garden. She picked some lettuce and put it in the new bag. Then off she went across the fields until she found a rabbit hole. She put the bag down with its mouth wide open so the lettuce could be seen. Then she hid herself behind a low hedge. Soon, a fat grey rabbit popped his head out of the hole. He smelled the fresh lettuce and jumped into the bag to

eat it. Puss-in-Boots leaped from behind the hedge and
swiftly drew the strings of the bag together and the fat rabbit
was caught.

Then Puss slung the bag over her shoulder and set off
in her yellow boots until she came to the King's palace. She
presented herself to the King, and bowing low said, "Your

Majesty, I have brought you a fat rabbit from the estate of my master, the Marquis of Carabas." The King was amused at the sight of a black cat in yellow boots, but he graciously accepted the gift. The next day Puss put a handful of grain

into her bag and went out to the fields. She set the bag as

before and lay down beside it

pretending to be dead.

This time two pheasants

came and started to eat the

grain. She waited for the right

moment, and quickly gathered up the strings of the bag,

catching both birds inside. Once more she set off for the

palace, and presented herself to the King."My master, the

Marquis of Carabas, begs your acceptance of these two

pheasants," said Puss-in Boots, bowing gracefully. "Tell your

master," said the King, "that I am pleased to accept his gift.

He must have a very fine estate." "Oh indeed, it is, very

fine," said Puss as she bowed and took her leave of the King.

As she passed through the great halls, she heard that the

King and his daughter were going to drive beside the river

that afternoon. Puss raced home to her master, and told him

about her visit to the palace, and then commanded him, "I

want you to go and swim in the river and if anyone asks your

name, you are to say that you are the Marquis of Carabas."

So he left Puss-in-Boots to guard his clothes and went and

swam in the river. Puss carefully hid the clothes under a pile

of stones, and waited for the royal carriage. As it

approached, Puss ran out, shouting, "Help! Help! The

Marquis of Carabas is drowning!" The King ordered the

coach to stop and sent his servants to rescue the Marquis.

Then Puss went up to the carriage, and with his hat in his

hand, bowed to the King and Princess and said, "We are indeed so grateful that you happened to be passing just now. But, alas, a thief has stolen my master's clothes."

The King sent a servant to the palace to get a suit, and when the miller's son put it on, he looked just like a prince. "This is my master, the Marquis of Carabas," said Puss to the King and Princess as she graciously introduced him. "We hope you will

drive on and dine with the Marquis."

"It will be a pleasure," replied the King, and

he invited the Marquis to ride in his carriage.

Puss ran ahead of the carriage and took a

short cut across the fields. Back on the road,

she came across some haymakers. They

stared at the sight of a black cat in yellow boots, and she told them sternly, "When the King passes this way and asks to whom this field of hay belongs, you are to say, 'To the Marquis of Carabas, your Majesty.' ."

Then she ran on until she came to a field where reapers were busy cutting the wheat. "When the King passes this way," said Puss, "and asks to whom this field of wheat belongs, you are to say, 'To the Marquis of Carabas, your Majesty.' ."

Now the land really belonged to a terrible Ogre, and Puss-in-Boots carried on running until she reached his great castle. No one ever visited him because he was so fright-

ening, but when he opened the door, Puss walked straight in,

showing off her fine boots. The Ogre was so shocked that he

could only stare at her. "I have heard that you can turn

yourself into a wild beast; is that true?" said Puss, calmly.

18

"Well naturally," said the Ogre swelling with pride, and then in a flash he became a roaring lion. Poor Puss ran and hid herself up the chimney!

The Ogre changed himself back again and laughed at Puss, who said, "It is truly wonderful that an Ogre such as yourself can become a great lion, but I very much doubt that you could change into a tiny creature, say, a mouse?" "Pooh! no problem at all," said the Ogre, and in an instant he had disappeared and Puss saw a tiny mouse running across the room. She pounced and seized the creature, and with one shake, the Ogre was gone forever.

At this moment, the King's carriage drew up outside

the castle. "You have a splendid estate," said the King to the miller's son, for sure enough, the haymakers and reapers had obeyed Puss, and told him the land belonged to the Marquis of Carabas; "And this is a magnificent castle."

They went inside and sat down to a feast.

"This young man would make a good husband

for my daughter," thought the King. "Your title does not match your wealth. I shall make you a Prince." The Princess loved the Prince, and he loved her. So they were married, and lived together happily in the Ogre's castle. Puss-in Boots lived in comfort to the end of her life and she never had to hunt again.